Robert Browning

So this then is Christmas eve

Robert Browning

So this then is Christmas eve

ISBN/EAN: 9783741193675

Manufactured in Europe, USA, Canada, Australia, Japa

Cover: Foto ©Andreas Hilbeck / pixelio.de

Manufactured and distributed by brebook publishing software
(www.brebook.com)

Robert Browning

So this then is Christmas eve

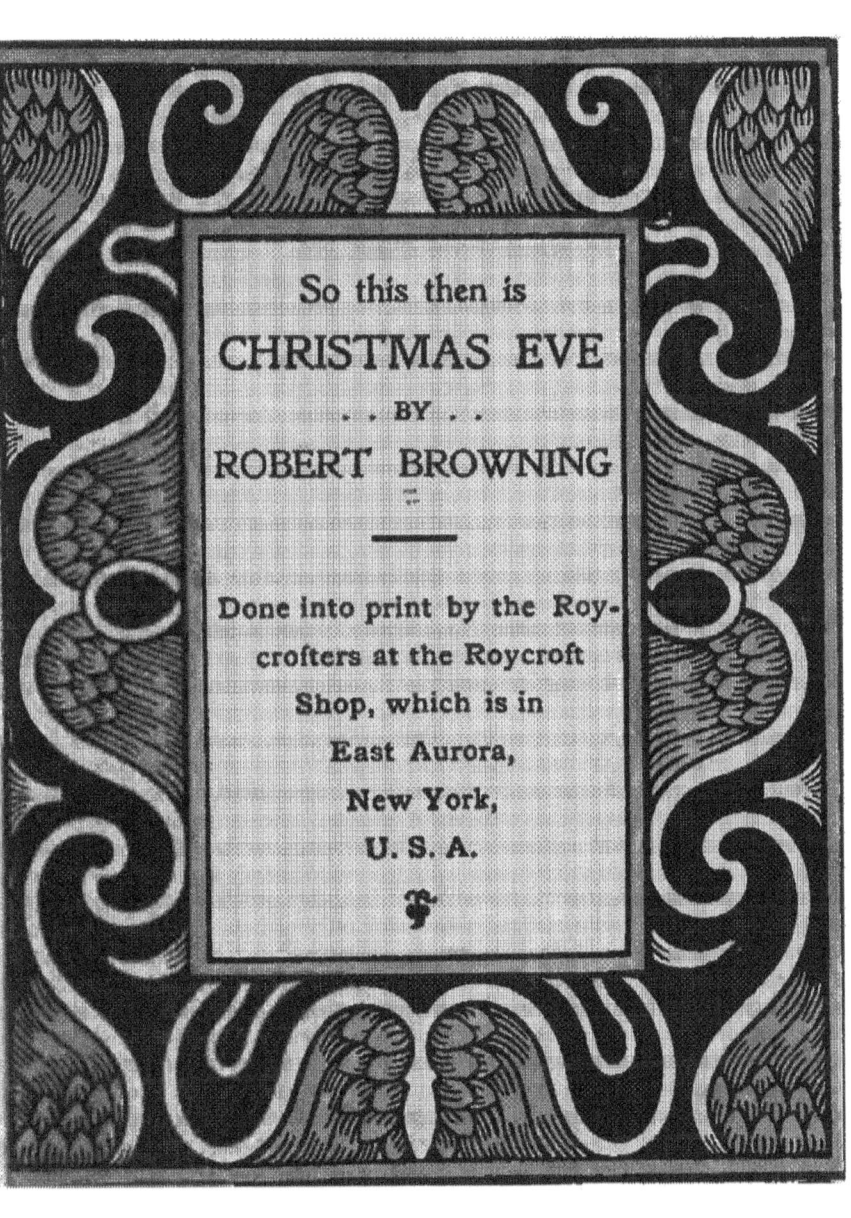

So this then is

CHRISTMAS EVE

. . BY . .

ROBERT BROWNING

———

Done into print by the Roy-
crofters at the Roycroft
Shop, which is in
East Aurora,
New York,
U. S. A.

INTRODUCTION

E find Robert Browning deeply religious, though he is never sanctimonious. Cant and ceremony, form without substance, anything that savors of falsity, is to his mind the unpardonable and death-dealing sin. ❧ At least, pure humor and true religiousness go hand in hand on this happy Christmas Eve, and neither is injured. The joyousness which bejewels everything at Christmas time sparkles all through the poem, as though the very angels had come from heaven to sing again with men. It is a very human song, and therefore a true one, handling with deepest insight the ludicrous, the unreal and the dishonest. It discovers the false as well as the true, first in the simple chapel service of the ignorant, next in the rainbow religion of the poet, and last in the emptiness of the rationalistic worship of a myth. It seeks and discovers the real, as the bee finds the honey.

The native intuitions of the human soul, the "primal elements" in man, are what Mr. Browning is always interested in and taking account of, whether found in the learned or the unlearned, in the rich or the poor. Whatever is real, Adham, Adam, Man, hu-man, this is what always contains depths and heights of interest for him. What he deplores and ridicules most of all is

i

the nullified man or woman, the inconsistent, the unnatural, the untrue.

"The soul, little else, is worth study," is a favorite quotation among Browning readers, taken from his introductory note to "Sordello." In whatsoever condition the soul is, it is still his immortal theme. "The Soul's Tragedy," to his mind, occurs, when all primal elements are filmed over by conventionalities, or by human wisdom, or by utilitarian considerations, until they have oozed away and no real personality is left. The fixedness of the soulless soul is what the author of "Christmas Eve" considers the most fearful and solemn death.

This poem is a narrative, and the narrator finds himself dodging a storm. He seeks to enter a little dissenting chapel, situated

> Where the town's bad blood once slept corruptly.

He snuggles himself up as closely as he can in the little four-by-six porch which serves as a doorway. He becomes interested in the different specimens of human nature that hurriedly and drippingly crowd past him to enter the door, the inner door, whose latch "grew more obstinate the more they fumbled."

"From the road, the lanes, or the common" they come; the stout, weary woman panting for breath, as she claps her umbrella, "a mere wreck of whalebones," down beside him; then the patient little sister-turned-mother, carrying the sickly babe on her breast

ii

(its one warm place), who stops to wring dry the drag-. gled ends of her shawl before she enters; then the dingy satins of a female something—all that is left of a woman; the coughing boy, etc., all of which goes to make up one of Browning's wonderful life-pictures ♣ "Very realistic," I suppose it might be called; vulgar perhaps; but one thing we may know: only the closest observer of the workings of the human soul could ever see all that our hero saw in this chapel door.

He finally enters with the rest. He is eyed as an inter-loper, indeed, yet there is no alternative. "The rain keeps driving," and at last Zion's chapel is filled and finds its flock all assembled, with "one sheep over."

Very rich is the study of this class of Christmas wor-shippers, which takes up the first three sections of the poem. Devout and very needy, we may notice, very humble, yet very sure of their ground, are they all. So safely housed do they seem that . . . "they front you as little disconcerted," as Lot might have marched, bound for the hills, with all wicked people behind him in Gomorrah ♣ They sniff the very dews of Hermon

> With such content in every snuffle,
> As the devil inside us loves to ruffle.

The old fat woman, as she listens to the sermon, purrs with pleasure; her thumbs twirl round and round each other as she maternally devours the pastor.

The "hot smell and the human noise," however, are soon too much for our intruder & he "flings out again."

A lull in the storm, & he takes a little by-path up to an eminence, where nature prepares for his more exquisite sensibilities a panorama of beauty. The "flying moon," with its shifting tints, touches with silver the rifts in the clouds. His head and limbs feel better, and he is glad that he has slipt the fetter, but, he says:

> My mind was full of the scene I had left.

That sermon! Such logic! The zeal and aspiration good,

> . . . Yet, fifty times over,
> Pharaoh received no demonstration,
> By his Baker's dream of Baskets Three,
> Of the doctrine of the Trinity.

Yet these people, no doubt, feel "a something," and this is the method of reproducing the mood, and it is a mood which strengthens by using. He sees that it is as the train was to him last week.

These lines were not lightly written by Mr. Browning, for here he touches upon his favorite theme, the contagion, transmission and power of personality.

However, this narrator will not be harsh, so he allows himself to meditate upon

> After how many modes, this Christmas Eve,
> Does the self-same weary thing take place?

how each form of worship goes on,

> Convincing to those convinced before.

Here is this ghastly truth again, this unchanging sequence of a chosen line or mode of life and thought. Always awful to Mr. Browning are the "streams of tendency." He never, like Matthew Arnold, would sub-

iv

stitute them for the Creator, although they sometimes
do "make for righteousness," since streams of tendency too often make for evil also.

Our genial hero, after indulging in good-natured med-
itation during his exquisite delight in nature, imagining
he has found through nature, nature's God, has a sudden arrest of thought, and more than thought, arrest
of life. He says at the moment when gazing

> With upturned eyes, I felt my brain
> Glutted with the glory

and it was during his most "ecstatic aquiescence,"
he "saw with terror" the Savior of men emerging from
that chapel with that same herd, and with His "face
averted," from him.

This whole poem reminds one of John G. Whittier's
"The Meeting." The theme is identical, but the method
of handling it is exactly characteristic of each poet.
One whose gentleness, as well as other qualities, has
made him great, treats of it in his gently powerful way ;
while the other with dramatic vigor, and with the very
fierceness of the judgment to come, makes one feel
like a sinner impelled for himself to cry out : "What
must I do to be saved?" yet with sparkling glints of
humor, which makes the follower of Christ feel the
serenest safety, does he make one to know

> God 's in his heaven,
> All 's well with the world.

🍀 With Mr. Browning's "Christmas Eve," there are

v

great Sinai-peaks ready to peal forth with awful thunder; in the very wide view of this great theme, there are whole ranges of mountain scenery, with valleys also lying in between them, all warm with the peace of their green pastures. Nothing is left out that the eye can take in. This is what makes Browning hard to read. It is as if one must travel, keeping one eye on the main points & peaks of thought while the other eye must traverse up and down hill and valley. The only way to get along at all, is to make a sort of mental leap, first from one main point to another, and then hold these, while, if there is any mental capacity left, one roams in and out, up and down, until the whole be taken in. If one trip will not suffice, it pays well to return and make the journey several times over, for new beauties always emerge.

A suggestion of the difference between Browning's "Christmas Eve," & Whittier's "The Meeting," may not be out of place then. Each poem has its loving and admiring readers, nor is it surprising if the same reader may greatly love to read both of these poems.

Browning's hero, on the verge of desolation, sees the error of his way, & repentantly remembers, "He did say, where two or three are met in My name, I will be in their midst." He sees he has despised Christ's friends, and begs to make amends. He makes confession that while he thought it best to worship in spirit and in truth and " in beauty," also, and not in " uncouth burlesque," he finds he must yet learn how dangerous it is to worship this Lord of All, in any other way than that of perfect humility. Whittier's same thought is thus expressed :

> God should be most where man is least ;
>
> .   .   .   .
>
> I lay the critic's glass aside,
> I tread upon my lettered pride,
> And, lowest-seated, testify
> To the oneness of humanity ;
>
> .   .   .   .
>
> He findeth not who seeks his own,
> The soul is lost that 's saved alone.

Our hero finally wins a full look from his Savior. Holding by the hem of His vesture, he visits other places of worship in a far different state of mind. He is suffused by a life and love that enlarges his vision. In losing his life he finds it. It is that

> Stoop of the soul which in bending upraises it too.

His new view of human need, and of Christ's love and pity, His saving love and pity, is a greater view than the one he had enjoyed alone upon his isolated mount of poetic vision, though the very heavens do declare to the sincere worshipper the glory of God. But all this glory of tint and of awful wonder had not revealed to him the glory of the Love incarnate in Christ ; yet none of it was lost upon him as it would have been upon a dumb and benumbed soul. So he carries it all in his heart, holding firm the hem of the garment, and with his Master visits other places of worship.

.   .   .   .

> We crossed the world—
> And what is this that rises
> This miraculous dome of God ?

They are at Rome, at St. Peter's great cathedral, where, it would seem that

> The angel's measuring-rod had meted
> What the sons of men completed.

It all seemed to be

> With arms wide open to embrace
> The entry of the human race.

Pomp of mass and trumpery of form did not keep the Savior, however, from finding what sincere love there was here.

> His eye detects a spark

and

> Discerns all ways open to reach him.

.   .   .   .

The narrator next finds himself making swift headway with

> Senses settling and steady with

.   .   .   .   ,   .

> My body caught up in the whirl and drift
> Of the vesture's amplitude.

Carried to a sort of temple, perhaps a college, he is left alone again, but for the garment's extreme edge, while the Master enters.

He finds that he is in Germany, in the quaint old town of Gottingen. The " high-cheek-boned " professor steps deliberately to his desk, because of his " cranium's overfreight," and with hoarse voice, and wan, weary look, with spectacles and notes adjusted, he begins his Christmas Eve discourse.

So rich and humorous, in smoothest diction, is this description of the professor and his audience, that it forms another of Mr. Browning's most wonderful life-like pictures.

His discourse is now to be weighed in the balance of our hearer's enlightened heart and mind. He came well-nigh losing hold on his hem in this place, however, so enchantingly liberal and realistic was it all. But he grasps firmly again the loving, living vesture, and is safe.

At last he finds himself sitting bolt upright again in the chapel, as if he had never left it, and as if he had never seen the "raree-show of Peter's successor" or "the laboratory of the professor;" but he had seen the Vision; "That was true."

> True as that heaven and earth exist.

There was the man with the wen on his neck, and the old fat woman evidently disgusted with this nodding guest. He also has a "ghostly warning" that the sermon is approaching its tenth head; so, after making notes of his dream, (though he does not tell us this, but what else could he have been doing with his pencil?) he says:

> I put up my pencil and join chorus
> To Hepzibah tune without further apology,

and sings

The seventeenth hymn in Whitfield's collection,
To conclude with the Doxology.

The companion poem to " Christmas Eve " is " Easter Day." They were written at Florence in 1850, when the author was thirty-eight years old, and were originally published under one title,—" Christmas Eve and Easter Day,—A Poem," in a volume by Chapman & Hall of London. Although allied in form and substance, each is a distinct poem. Each lays hold of the day which its name indicates, and is lived in the profoundest experience through the vision of the Christ. Mr. Browning sat for some years under the ministry of a Congregationalist, one Rev. Thomas Jones, an able and eloquent Welshman. It is not unlikely that his sincere mind and heart here witnessed things that neither the " raree-show " of Papacy, nor the rationalism of the day, nor the form of the Established Church itself, knew much about, while, no doubt, he found much to satisfy his own emotional rationalistic thirst for true life.

It is not rash to conclude that in this poem the author's own " soul-depths boil in earnest," for its teachings are in accord with his well-known views of Christianity. It is most significant when we remember his mother, Sarianna Wiedeman, was " in religion a Christian, a devout Congregationalist."

                                        MARY H. HULL.

x

CHRISTMAS EVE

Florence—1850

I

UT of the little chapel I burst
Into the fresh night-air again.
Five minutes full, I waited first
In the doorway, to escape the
      rain
That drove in gusts down the
      common's center
At the edge of which the chapel stands,
Before I plucked up heart to enter.
Heaven knows how many sorts of hands
Reached past me, groping for the latch
Of the inner door that hung on catch
More obstinate the more they fumbled,
Till, giving way at last with a scold
Of the crazy hinge, in squeezed or tumbled
One sheep more to the rest in fold,
And left me irresolute, standing sentry
In the sheepfold's lath-and-plaster entry,
Six feet long by three feet wide,

Partitioned off from the vast inside—
I blocked up half of it at least.
No remedy ; the rain kept driving.
They eyed me much as some wild beast,
That congregation, still arriving,
Some of them by the main road, white
A long way past me into the night,
Skirting the common, then diverging;
Not a few suddenly emerging
From the common's self through the paling
    gaps,
—They house in the gravel-pits perhaps,
Where the road stops short with its safeguard
    border
Of lamps, as tired of such disorder ;—
But the most turned in yet more abruptly
From a certain squalid knot of alleys,
Where the town's bad blood once slept cor-
    ruptly,
Which now the little chapel rallies
And leads into day again, —its priestliness
Lending itself to hide their beastliness
So cleverly (thanks in part to the mason),
And putting so cheery a whitewashed face on
Those neophytes too much in lack of it,

That, where you cross the common as I did,
And meet the party thus presided,
" Mount Zion " with Love-lane at the back
    of it,
They front you as little disconcerted
As, bound for the hills, her fate averted,
And her wicked people made to mind him,
Lot might have marched with Gomorrah
    behind him.

 ELL, from the road, the lanes or
the common,
In came the flock : the fat weary
woman,
Panting and bewildered, down-
clapping
Her umbrella with a mighty report,
Grounded it by me, wry and flapping,
A wreck of whalebones ; then, with a snort,
Like a startled horse, at the interloper
(Who humbly knew himself improper,
But could not shrink up small enough)
—Round to the door, and in,—the gruff
Hinge's invariable scold
Making my very blood run cold.
Prompt in the wake of her, up-pattered
On broken clogs, the many-tattered
Little old-faced peaking sister-turned-mother
Of the sickly babe she tried to smother
Somehow up, with its spotted face,
From the cold, on her breast, the one warm
place ;
She too must stop, wring the poor ends dry
Of a draggled shawl, and add thereby

Her tribute to the door-mat, sopping
Already from my own clothes' dropping,
Which yet she seemed to grudge I should
    stand on :
Then, stooping down to take off her pattens,
She bore them defiantly, in each hand one,
Planted together before her breast
And its babe, as good as a lance in rest.
Close on her heels, the dingy satins
Of a female something, past me flitted,
With lips as much too white, as a streak
Lay far too red on each hollow cheek
And it seemed the very door-hinge pitied
All that was left of a woman once,
Holding at least its tongue for the nonce.
Then a tall yellow man, like the Penitent Thief,
With his jaw bound up in a handkerchief,
And eyelids screwed together tight,
Led himself in by some inner light.
And, except from him, from each that entered,
I got the same interrogation—
" What, you the alien, you have ventured
To take with us, the elect, your station ?
A carer for none of it, a Gallio ! "—
Thus, plain as print, I read the glance

At a common prey, in each countenance
As of huntsman giving his hounds the tallyho.
And when the door's cry drowned their
    wonder,
The draught, it always sent in shutting,
Made the flame of the single tallow candle
In the cracked square lantern I stood under,
Shoot its blue lip at me, rebutting
As it were, the luckless cause of scandal :
I verily fancied the zealous light
(In the chapel's secret, too !) for spite
Would shudder itself clean off the wick,
With the airs of a Saint John's Candlestick.
There was no standing it much longer.
" Good folks," thought I, as resolve grew
    stronger,
" This way you perform the Grand-Inquisitor
When the weather sends you a chance visitor ?
You are the men, and wisdom shall die with
    you,
And none of the old Seven Churches vie with
    you !
But still, despite the pretty perfection
To which you carry your trick of exclusiveness,
And taking God's word under wise protection,

Correct its tendency to diffusiveness,
And bid one reach it over hot ploughshares,—
Still, as I say, though you 've found salvation,
If I should choose to cry, as now, ' Shares ! '—
See if the best of you bars me my ration !
I prefer, if you please, for my expounder
Of the laws of the feast, the feast's own
     Founder ;
Mine 's the same right with your poorest and
     sickliest,
Supposing I don the marriage vestiment :
So, shut your mouth and open your Testament,
And carve me my portion at your quickliest! "
Accordingly, as a shoemaker's lad
With wizened face in want of soap,
And wet apron wound round his waist like a
     rope,
(After stopping outside, for his cough was bad,
To get the fit over, poor gentle creature,
And so avoid disturbing the preacher)
—Passed in, I sent my elbow spikewise
At the shutting door, and entered likewise,
Received the hinge's accustomed greeting,
And crossed the threshold's magic pentacle,
And found myself in full conventicle,

—To wit, in Zion Chapel Meeting,
On the Christmas Eve of 'Forty-nine,
Which, calling its flock to their special clover,
Found all assembled and one sheep over,
Whose lot, as the weather pleased, was mine.

III

VERY soon had enough of it.
The hot smell & the human noises,
And my neighbor's coat, the
    greasy cuff of it,
Were a pebble-stone that a child's
    hand poises,
Compared with the pig-of-lead-like pressure
Of the preaching man's immense stupidity,
As he poured his doctrine forth, full measure,
To meet his audience's avidity.
You needed not the wit of the Sibyl
To guess the cause of it all, in a twinkling:
No sooner our friend had got an inkling
Of treasure hid in the Holy Bible,
(Whene'er 't was the thought first struck him,
How death, at unawares, might duck him
Deeper than the grave, and quench
The gin-shop's light in hell's grim drench)
Than he handled it so, in fine irreverence,
As to hug the book of books to pieces:
And, a patchwork of chapters and texts in
    severance,
Not improved by the private dog's-ears and
    creases,

19

Having clothed his own soul with, he 'd fair
    see equipt yours,—
So tossed you again your Holy Scriptures.
And you picked them up, in a sense, no doubt:
Nay, had but a single face of my neighbors
Appeared to suspect that the preacher's labor
Were help which the world could be saved
    without,
'T is odds but I might have borne in quiet
A qualm or two at my spiritual diet,
Or (who can tell?) perchance even mustered
Somewhat to urge in behalf of the sermon:
But the flock sat on, divinely flustered,
Sniffing, methought, its dew of Hermon
With such content in every snuffle,
As the devil inside us loves to ruffle.
My old fat woman purred with pleasure,
And thumb round thumb went twirling faster
While she, to his periods keeping measure,
Maternally devoured the pastor.
The man with the handkerchief untied it,
Showed us a horrible wen inside it,
Gave his eyelids yet another screwing,
And rocked himself as the woman was doing
The shoemaker's lad, discreetly choking,

Kept down his cough. 'T was too provoking!
My gorge rose at the nonsense and stuff of it;
So, saying like Eve when she plucked the
     apple,
"I wanted a taste, and now there 's enough
     of it,"
I flung out of the little chapel.

IV

HERE was a lull in the rain, a lull
In the wind too ; the moon was risen,
And would have shone out pure and full,
But for the ramparted cloud-prison,
Block on block built up in the West,
For what purpose the wind knows best,
Who changes his mind continually.
And the empty other half of the sky
Seemed in its silence as if it knew
What, any moment, might look through
A chance gap in that fortress massy :—
Through its fissures you got hints
Of the flying moon, by the shifting tints,
Now, a dull lion-color, now, brassy
Burning to yellow, and whitest yellow,
Like furnace-smoke just ere flames bellow,
All a-simmer with intense strain
To let her through,—then blank again,
At the hope of her appearance failing.
Just by the chapel, a break in the railing
Shows a narrow path directly across;

'T is ever dry walking there, on the moss—
Besides, you go gently all the way up-hill.
I stooped under and soon felt better ;
My head grew lighter, my limbs more supple,
As I walked on, glad to have slipt the fetter.
My mind was full of the scene I had left,
That placid flock, that pastor vociferant,
—How this outside was pure and different!
The sermon, now—what a mingled weft
Of good and ill! Were either less,
Its fellow had colored the whole distinctly ;
But alas for the excellent earnestness,
And the truths, quite true if stated succinctly;
But as surely false, in their quaint present-
    ment,
However to pastor and flock's contentment !
Say rather, such truths looked false to your
    eyes,
With his provings and parallels twisted and
    twined,
Till how could you know them, grown double
    their size
In the natural fog of the good man's mind,
Like yonder spots of our roadside lamps,
Haloed about with the common's damps?

Truth remains true, the fault 's in the prover;
The zeal was good, and the aspiration;
And yet, and yet, yet, fifty times over,
Pharaoh received no demonstration,
By his Baker's dream of Baskets Three,
Of the doctrine of the Trinity,—
Although, as our preacher thus embellished it,
Apparently his hearers relished it
With so unfeigned a gust—who knows if
They did not prefer our friend to Joseph?
But so it is everywhere, one way with all of
     them!
These people have really felt, no doubt,
A something, the motion they style the Call
     of them;
And this is their method of bringing about,
By a mechanism of words and tones,
(So many texts in so many groans)
A sort of reviving and reproducing,
More or less perfectly, (who can tell?)
The mood itself, which strengthens by using;
And how that happens, I understand well.
A tune was born in my head last week,
Out of the thump-thump and shriek-shriek

Of the train, as I came by it, up from
    Manchester ;
And when, next week, I take it back again,
My head will sing to the engine's clack again,
While it only makes my neighbor's haunches
    stir,
—Finding no dormant musical sprout
In him, as in me, to be jolted out.
'T is the taught already that profits by
    teaching ;
He gets no more from the railway's preaching
Than, from this preacher who does the rail's
    office, I :
Whom therefore the flock cast a jealous eye on.
Still, why paint over their door "Mount Zion,"
To which all flesh shall come, saith the
    prophecy ?

V

UT wherefore be harsh on a
    single case ?
After how many modes, this
    Christmas Eve,
Does the self-same weary thing
    take place ?
The same endeavor to make you believe,
And with much the same effect, no more :
Each method abundantly convincing,
As I say, to those convinced before,
But scarce to be swallowed without wincing
By the not-as-yet-convinced. For me,
I have my own church equally :
And in this church my faith sprang first !
(I said, as I reached the rising ground,
And the wind began again, with a burst
Of rain in my face, and a glad rebound
From the heart beneath, as if, God speeding me,
I entered his church-door, nature leading me)
—In youth I looked to these very skies,
And probing their immensities,
I found God there, his visible power ;
Yet felt in my heart, amid all its sense
Of the power, an equal evidence

That his love, there too, was the nobler dower.
For the loving worm within its clod
Were diviner than a loveless god
Amid his worlds, I will dare to say.
You know what I mean : God 's all, man 's
    nought :
But also, God, whose pleasure brought
Man into being, stands away
As it were a handbreadth off, to give
Room for the newly-made to live,
And look at him from a place apart,
And use his gifts of brain and heart,
Given, indeed, but to keep forever.
Who speaks of man, then, must not sever
Man's very elements from man,
Saying, " But all is God's "—whose plan
Was to create man and then leave him
Able, his own word saith, to grieve him,
But able to glorify him too,
As a mere machine could never do,
That prayed or praised, all unaware
Of its fitness for aught but praise and prayer,
Made perfect as a thing of course.
Man, therefore, stands on his own stock
Of love and power as a pin-point rock :

And, looking to God who ordained divorce
Of the rock from his boundless continent,
Sees, in his power made evident,
Only excess by a million-fold
O'er the power God gave man in the mould.
For, note: man's hand, first formed to carry
A few pounds' weight, when taught to marry
Its strength with an engine's, lifts a mountain,
—Advancing in power by one degree;
And why count steps through eternity?
But love is the ever-springing fountain:
Man may enlarge or narrow his bed
For the water's play, but the water-head—
How can he multiply or reduce it?
As easy create it, as cause it to cease;
He may profit by it, or abuse it,
But 't is not a thing to bear increase
As power does: be love less or more
In the heart of man, he keeps it shut
Or opes it wide, as he pleases, but
Love's sum remains what it was before.
So, gazing up, in my youth, at love
As seen through power, ever above
All modes which make it manifest,
My soul brought all to a single test—

That he, the Eternal First and Last,
Who, in his power, had so surpassed
All man conceives of what is might,—
Whose wisdom, too, showed infinite,
—Would prove as infinitely good ;
Would never, (my soul understood,)
With power to work all love desires,
Bestow e'en less than man requires ;
That he who endlessly was teaching,
Above my spirit's utmost reaching,
What love can do in the leaf or stone,
(So that to master this alone,
This done in the stone or leaf for me,
I must go on learning endlessly)
Would never need that I, in turn,
Should point him out defect unheeded,
And show that God had yet to learn
What the meanest human creature needed,
—Not life, to wit, for a few short years,
Tracking his way through doubts and fears,
While the stupid earth on which I stay
Suffers no change, but passive adds
Its myriad years to myriads,
Though I, he gave it to, decay,
Seeing death come and choose about me,

And my dearest ones depart without me.
No : love which, on earth, amid all the shows
    of it,
Has ever been seen the sole good of life in it
The love, ever growing there, spite of the
    strife in it,
Shall arise, made perfect, from death's repose
    of it.
And I shall behold thee, face to face,
O God, and in thy light retrace
How in all I loved here, still wast thou !
Whom pressing to, then, as I fain would now,
I shall find as able to satiate
The love, thy gift, as my spirit's wonder
Thou art able to quicken and sublimate,
With this sky of thine, that I now walk under,
And glory in thee for, as I gaze
Thus, thus ! Oh, let men keep their ways
Of seeking thee in a narrow shrine—
Be this my way ! And this is mine !

VI

OR lo, what think you ? suddenly
The rain and the wind ceased,
    and the sky
Received at once the full fruition
Of the moon's consummate
    apparition.
The black cloud-barricade was riven,
Ruined beneath her feet, and driven
Deep in the West ; while, bare and breathless,
North and South and East lay ready
For a glorious thing that, dauntless, deathless,
Sprang across them and stood steady.
'T was a moon-rainbow, vast and perfect,
From heaven to heaven extending, perfect
As the mother-moon's self, full in face.
It rose, distinctly at the base
With its seven proper colors chorded,
Which still, in the rising, were compressed,
Until at last they coalesced,
And supreme the spectral creature lorded
In a triumph of whitest white,—
Above which intervened the night.
But above night too, like only the next,
The second of a wondrous sequence,

31

Reaching in rare and rarer frequence,
Till the heaven of heavens were circumflexed
Another rainbow rose, a mightier,
Fainter, flushier and flightier,—
Rapture dying along its verge.
Oh, whose foot shall I see emerge,
Whose, from the straining topmost dark,
On to the keystone of that arc ?

VII

THIS sight was shown me, there
    and then,—
Me, one out of a world of men,
Singled forth, as the chance
    might hap
To another if, in a thunderclap
Where I heard noise and you saw flame,
Some one man knew God called his
    name.
For me, I think I said, "Appear!
Good were it to be ever here.
If thou wilt, let me build to thee
Service-tabernacles three,
Where, forever in thy presence,
In ecstatic acquiescence,
Far alike from thriftless learning
And ignorance's undiscerning,
I may worship and remain!"
Thus at the show above me, gazing
With upturned eyes, I felt my brain
Glutted with the glory, blazing
Throughout its whole mass, over and
    under,
Until at length it burst asunder

The too-much glory, as it seemed,
Passing from out me to the ground,
Then palely serpentining round
Into the dark with mazy error.

VIII

LL at once I looked up with
 terror.
He was there.
He himself with his human air,
On the narrow pathway, just
 before.
I saw the back of him, no more—
He had left the chapel, then, as I.
I forgot all about the sky.
No face : only the sight
Of a sweepy garment, vast and white,
With a hem that I could recognize.
I felt terror, no surprise ;
My mind filled with the cataract
At one bound of the mighty fact.
"I remember, he did say
Doubtless that, to this world's end,
Where two or three should meet and pray,
He would be in the midst, their friend ;
Certainly he was there with them ! "
And my pulses leaped for joy
Of the golden thought without alloy,
That I saw his very vesture's hem.
Then rushed the blood back, cold and clear,

With a fresh enhancing shiver of fear ;
And I hastened, cried out while I pressed
To the salvation of the vest,
" But not so, Lord ! It cannot be
That thou, indeed, art leaving me—
Me, that have despised thy friends !
Did my heart make no amends ?
Thou art the love of God—above
His power, didst hear me place his love,
And that was leaving the world for thee.
Therefore thou must not turn from me
As I had chosen the other part !
Folly and pride o'ercame my heart.
Our best is bad, nor bears thy test ;
Still, it should be our very best.
I thought it best that thou, the spirit,
Be worshipped in spirit and in truth,
And in beauty, as even we require it—
Not in the forms burlesque, uncouth,
I left but now, as scarcely fitted
For thee : I knew not what I pitied.
But, all I felt there, right or wrong,
What is it to thee, who curest sinning ?
Am I not weak as thou art strong ?
I have looked to thee from the beginning,

Straight up to thee through all the world
Which, like an idle scroll, lay furled
To nothingness on either side:
And since the time thou wast descried,
Spite of the weak heart, so have I
Lived ever, and so fain would die,
Living and dying, thee before!
But if thou leavest me "—

IX

ESS or more,
I suppose that I spoke thus.
When,—have mercy, Lord, on
　　us !
The whole face turned upon me
　　full.
And I spread myself beneath it,
As when the bleacher spreads, to seethe it
In the cleansing sun, his wool,—
Steeps in the flood of noontide whiteness
Some defiled, discolored web—
So lay I, saturate with brightness.
And when the flood appeared to ebb,
Lo, I was walking, light and swift,
With my senses settling fast and steadying,
But my body caught up in the whirl and drift
Of the vesture's amplitude, still eddying
On, just before me, still to be followed,
As it carried me after with its motion :
What shall I say ?—as a path were hollowed
And a man went weltering through the ocean,
Sucked along in the flying wake
Of the luminous water-snake.
Darkness and cold were cloven, as through

I passed, upborne yet walking too.
And I turned to myself at intervals,—
"So he said, so it befalls.
God who registers the cup
Of mere cold water, for his sake
To a disciple rendered up,
Disdains not his own thirst to slake
At the poorest love was ever offered :
And because my heart I proffered,
With true love trembling at the brim,
He suffers me to follow him
Forever, my own way,—dispensed
From seeking to be influenced
By all the less immediate ways
That earth, in worships manifold,
Adopts to reach, by prayer and praise,
The garment's hem, which, lo, I hold ! "

X

ND so we crossed the world and
    stopped.
For where am I, in city or plain,
Since I am 'ware of the world
    again ?
And what is this that rises
    propped
With pillars of prodigious girth ?
Is it really on the earth,
This miraculous Dome of God ?
Has the angel's measuring-rod
Which numbered cubits, gem from gem,
'Twixt the gates of the New Jerusalem,
Meted it out,—and what he meted,
Have the sons of men completed ?
—Binding, ever as he bade,
Columns in the colonnade
With arms wide open to embrace
The entry of the human race
To the breast of . . . what is it, yon building,
Ablaze in front, all paint and gilding,
With marble for brick, and stones of price
For garniture of the edifice ?
Now I see ; it is no dream ;

It stands there and it does not seem :
Forever, in pictures, thus it looks,
And thus I have read of it in books
Often in England, leagues away,
And wondered how these fountains play,
Growing up eternally
Each to a musical water-tree,
Whose blossoms drop, a glittering boon,
Before my eyes, in the light of the moon,
To the granite lavers underneath.
Liar and dreamer in your teeth !
I, the sinner that speak to you,
Was in Rome this night, and stood, and
    knew
Both this and more. For see, for see,
The dark is rent, mine eye is free
To pierce the crust of the outer wall,
And I view inside, and all there, all,
As the swarming hollow of a hive,
The whole Basilica alive !
Men in the chancel, body and nave,
Men on the pillars' architrave,
Men on the statues, men on the tombs
With popes and kings in their porphyry
    wombs,

All famishing in expectation
Of the main-altar's consummation.
For see, for see, the rapturous moment
Approaches, and earth's best endowment
Blends with heaven's; the taper-fires
Pant up, the winding brazen spires
Heave loftier yet the baldachin;
The incense-gaspings, long kept in,
Suspire in clouds; the organ blatant
Holds his breath and grovels latent,
As if God's hushing finger grazed him,
(Like Behemoth when he praised him)
At the silver bell's shrill tinkling,
Quick cold drops of terror sprinkling
On the sudden pavement strewed
With faces of the multitude.
Earth breaks up, time drops away,
In flows heaven, with its new day
Of endless life, when He who trod,
Very man and very God,
This earth in weakness, shame and pain,
Dying the death whose signs remain
Up yonder on the accursed tree,—
Shall come again, no more to be
Of captivity the thrall,

But the one God, All in all,
King of kings, Lord of lords,
As His servant John received the words,
" I died, and live forevermore ! "

XI

ET I was left outside the door.
"Why sit I here on the threshold-
stone,
Left till He return, alone
Save for the garment's extreme
fold
Abandoned still to bless my hold?"
My reason, to my doubt, replied,
As if a book were opened wide,
And at a certain page I traced
Every record undefaced,
Added by successive years,—
The harvestings of truth's stray ears
Singly gleaned, and in one sheaf
Bound together for belief.
Yes, I said—that he will go
And sit with these in turn, I know.
Their faith's heart beats, though her head
swims
Too giddily to guide her limbs,
Disabled by their palsy-stroke
From propping mine. Though Rome's gross
yoke
Drops off, no more to be endured,

Her teaching is not so obscured
By errors and perversities,
That no truth shines athwart the lies :
And he, whose eye detects a spark
Even where, to man's, the whole seems dark,
May well see flame where each beholder
Acknowledges the embers smoulder.
But I, a mere man, fear to quit
The clue God gave me as most fit
To guide my footsteps through life's maze,
Because himself discerns all ways
Open to reach him : I, a man
Able to mark where faith began
To swerve aside, till from its summit
Judgment drops her damning plummet,
Pronouncing such a fatal space
Departed from the founder's base :
He will not bid me enter too,
But rather sit, as now I do,
Awaiting his return outside.
—'T was thus my reason straight replied
And joyously I turned, and pressed
The garment's skirt upon my breast,
Until, afresh its light suffusing me,
My heart cried—" What has been abusing me

That I should wait here lonely and coldly,
Instead of rising, entering boldly,
Baring truth's face, and letting drift
Her veils of lies as they choose to shift ?
Do these men praise him ? I will raise
My voice up to their point of praise !
I see the error ; but above
The scope of error, see the love.—
Oh, love of those first Christian days !
—Fanned so soon into a blaze,
From the spark preserved by the trampled sect,
That the antique sovereign Intellect
Which then sat ruling in the world,
Like a change in dreams, was hurled
From the throne he reigned upon :
You looked up and he was gone.
Gone, his glory of the pen !
—Love, with Greece and Rome in ken,
Bade her scribes abhor the trick
Of poetry and rhetoric,
And exult with hearts set free,
In blessed imbecility
Scrawled, perchance, on some torn sheet
Leaving Sallust incomplete.
Gone, his pride of sculptor, painter !

—Love, while able to acquaint her
While the thousand statues yet
Fresh from chisel, pictures wet
From brush, she saw on every side,
Chose rather with an infant's pride
To frame those portents which impart
Such unction to true Christian Art.
Gone, music too! The air was stirred
By happy wings: Terpander's bird
(That, when the cold came, fled away)
Would tarry not the wintry day,—
As more-enduring sculpture must,
Till filthy saints rebuked the gust
With which they chanced to get a sight
Of some dear naked Aphrodite
They glanced a thought above the toes of,
By breaking zealously her nose off.
Love, surely, from that music's lingering,
Might have filched her organ-fingering,
Nor chosen rather to set prayings
To hog-grunts, praises to horse-neighings.
Love was the startling thing, the new:
Love was the all-sufficient too;
And seeing that, you see the rest:
As a babe can find its mother's breast

As well in darkness as in light,
Love shut our eyes, and all seemed right.
True, the world's eyes are open now :
—Less need for me to disallow
Some few that keep Love's zone unbuckled,
Peevish as ever to be suckled,
Lulled by the same old baby-prattle
With intermixture of the rattle,
When she would have them creep, stand steady
Upon their feet, or walk already,
Not to speak of trying to climb.
I will be wise another time,
And not desire a wall between us,
When next I see a church-roof cover
So many species of one genus,
All with foreheads bearing lover
Written above the earnest eyes of them ;
All with breasts that beat for beauty,
Whether sublimed, to the surprise of them,
In noble daring, steadfast duty,
The heroic in passion, or in action,—
Or, lowered for sense's satisfaction,
To the mere outside of human creatures,
Mere perfect form and faultless features.
What ? with all Rome here, whence to levy

Such contributions to their appetite,
With women and men in a gorgeous bevy,
They take, as it were, a padlock, clap it tight
On their southern eyes, restrained from feeding
On the glories of their ancient reading,
On the beauties of their modern singing,
On the wonders of the builder's bringing,
On the majesties of Art around them,—
And all these loves, late struggling incessant,
When faith has at last united and bound them,
They offer up to God for a present?
Why, I will, on the whole, be rather proud
    of it,—
And only taking the act in reference
To the other recipients who might have
    allowed it,
I will rejoice that God had the preference."

XII

O I summed up my new resolves:
Too much love there can never be.
And where the intellect devolves
Its function on love exclusively,
I, a man who possesses both,
Will accept the provision, noth-
    ing loth,
—Will feast my love, then depart elsewhere,
That my intellect may find its share.
And ponder, O soul, the while thou departest,
And see thou applaud the great heart of the
    artist,
Who, examining the capabilities
Of the block of marble he has to fashion
Into a type of thought or passion,—
Not always, using obvious facilities,
Shapes it, as any artist can,
Into a perfect symmetrical man,
Complete from head to foot of the life-size,
Such as old Adam stood in his wife's eyes,—
But, now and then, bravely aspires to con-
    summate
A Colossus by no means so easy to come at,
And uses the whole of his block for the bust,

Leaving the mind of the public to finish it,
Since cut it ruefully short he must:
On the face alone he expends his devotion,
He rather would mar than resolve to diminish it.
—Saying, " Applaud me for this grand notion
Of what a face may be! As for completing it
In breast and body and limbs, do that, you!"
All hail! I fancy how, happily meeting it,
A trunk and legs would perfect the statue,
Could man carve so as to answer volition.
And how much nobler than petty cavils,
Were a hope to find, in my spirit-travels,
Some artist of another ambition,
Who having a block to carve, no bigger,
Has spent his power on the opposite quest,
And believed to begin at the feet was best—
For so may I see, ere I die, the whole figure!

XIII

O sooner said than out in the
    night!
My heart beat lighter and more
    light:
And still, as before, I was walk-
    ing swift,
With my senses settling fast and steadying,
But my body caught up in the whirl and drift
Of the vesture's amplitude, still eddying
On just before me, still to be followed,
As it carried me after with its motion,
—What shall I say?—as a path were hollowed,
And a man went weltering through the ocean,
Sucked along in the flying wake
Of the luminous water-snake.

XIV

LONE! I am left alone once
     more—
(Save for the garment's extreme
     fold
Abandoned still to bless my hold)
Alone, beside the entrance-door
Of a sort of temple,—perhaps a college,
—Like nothing I ever saw before
At home in England, to my knowledge.
The tall old quaint irregular town!
It may be . . . though which, I can't affirm
     . . . any
Of the famous middle-age towns of Germany;
And this flight of stairs where I sit down,
Is it Halle, Weimar, Cassel, Frankfort,
Or Gottingen, I have to thank for 't?
It may be Gottingen,—most likely.
Through the open door I catch obliquely
Glimpses of a lecture-hall;
And not a bad assembly neither,
Ranged decent and symmetrical
On benches, waiting what 's to see there;
Which, holding still by the vesture's hem,
I also resolve to see with them,

Cautious this time how I suffer to slip
The chance of joining in fellowship
With any that call themselves his friends ;
As these folks do, I have a notion.
But hist—a buzzing and emotion !
All settle themselves, the while ascends
By the creaking rail to the lecture-desk,
Step by step, deliberate
Because of his cranium's over-freight,
Three parts sublime to one grotesque,
If I have proved an accurate guesser,
The hawk-nosed, high-cheekboned Professor.
I felt at once as if there ran
A shoot of love from my heart to the man—
That sallow virgin-minded studious
Martyr to mild enthusiasm,
As he uttered a kind of cough-preludious
That woke my sympathetic spasm,
(Beside some spitting that made me sorry)
And stood, surveying his auditory
With a wan pure look, wellnigh celestial,—
Those blue eyes had survived so much !
While, under the foot they could not smutch,
Lay all the fleshly and the bestial.
Over he bowed, and arranged his notes,

Till the auditory's clearing of throats
Was done with, died into a silence;
And when each glance was upward sent,
Each bearded mouth composed intent,
And a pin might be heard drop half a mile
    hence,—
He pushed back higher his spectacles,
Let the eyes stream out like lamps from cells,
And giving his head of hair—a hake
Of undressed tow, for color and quantity—
One rapid and impatient shake,
(As our own young England adjusts a jaunty
    tie
When about to impart, on mature digestion,
Some thrilling view of the surplice-question)
—The Professor's grave voice, sweet though
    hoarse,
Broke into his Christmas Eve discourse.

XV

ND he began it by observing
How reason dictated that men
Should rectify the natural swerv-
    ing,
By a reversion, now and then,
To the well-heads of knowledge, few
And far away, whence rolling grew
The life-stream wide whereat we drink,
Commingled, as we needs must think,
With waters alien to the source;
To do which, aimed this eve's discourse;
Since, where could be a fitter time
For tracing backward to its prime,
This Christianity, this lake,
This reservoir, whereat we slake,
From one or other bank, our thirst?
So, he proposed inquiring first
Into the various sources whence
This Myth of Christ is derivable;
Demanding from the evidence,
(Since plainly no such life was livable)
How these phenomena should class?
Whether 't were best opine Christ was,

Or never was at all, or whether
He was and was not, both together—
It matters little for the name,
So the idea be left the same.
Only, for practical purpose' sake,
'T was obviously as well to take
The popular story,—understanding
How the ineptitude of the time,
And the penman's prejudice, expanding
Fact into fable fit for the clime,
Had, by slow and sure degrees, translated it
Into this myth, this Individuum,—
Which, when reason had strained and abated
    it
Of foreign matter, left, for residuum,
A Man !—a right true man, however,
Whose work was worthy a man's endeavor :
Work, that gave warrant almost sufficient
To his disciples, for rather believing
He was just omnipotent and omniscient,
As it gives to us, for as frankly receiving
His word, their tradition,—which, though it
    meant
Something entirely different
From all that those who only heard it,

In their simplicity thought and averred it,
Had yet a meaning quite as respectable :
For, among other doctrines delectable,
Was he not surely the first to insist on
The natural sovereignty of our race ?—
Here the lecturer came to a pausing-place.
And while his cough, like a droughty piston,
Tried to dislodge the husk that grew to him,
I seized the occasion of bidding adieu to him,
The vesture still within my hand.

XVI

COULD interpret its command.
This time he would not bid me
    enter
The exhausted air-bell of the
    Critic.
Truth's atmosphere may grow
    mephitic
When Papist struggles with Dissenter,
Impregnating its pristine clarity,
—One, by his daily fare's vulgarity,
Its gust of broken meat and garlic ;
—One, by his soul's too-much presuming
To turn the frankincense's fuming
And vapors of the candle starlike
Into the cloud her wings she buoys on.
Each, that thus sets the pure air seething,
May poison it for healthy breathing—
But the Critic leaves no air to poison;
Pumps out with ruthless ingenuity
Atom by atom, and leaves you—vacuity.
Thus much of Christ does he reject ?
And what retain ? His intellect ?
What is it I must reverence duly ?
Poor intellect for worship, truly,

59

Which tells me simply what was told
(If mere morality, bereft
Of the God in Christ, be all that 's left)
Elsewhere by voices manifold;
With this advantage, that the stater
Made nowise the important stumble
Of adding, he, the sage and humble,
Was also one with the Creator.
You urge Christ's followers' simplicity:
But how does shifting blame evade it?
Have wisdom's words no more felicity?
The stumbling-block, his speech—who laid it?
How comes it that for one found able
To sift the truth of it from fable,
Millions believe it to the letter?
Christ's goodness, then—does that fare better?
Strange goodness, which upon the score
Of being goodness, the mere due
Of man to fellow-man, much more
To God—should take another view
Of its possessor's privilege,
And bid him rule his race! You pledge
Your fealty to such rule? What, all—
From heavenly John and Attic Paul,
And that brave weather-battered Peter,

Whose stout faith only stood completer
For buffets, sinning to be pardoned,
As, more his hands hauled nets, they hardened,
All, down to you, the man of men,
Professing here at Gottingen,
Compose Christ's flock! They, you and I,
Are sheep of a good man! And why?
The goodness,—how did he acquire it?
Was it self-gained, did God inspire it?
Choose which; then tell me, on what ground
Should its possessor dare propound
His claim to rise o'er us an inch?
Were goodness all some man's invention,
Who arbitrarily made mention
What we should follow, and whence flinch,—
What qualities might take the style
Of right and wrong,—and had such guessing
Met with as general acquiescing
As graced the alphabet erewhile,
When A got leave an Ox to be,
No Camel (quoth the Jews) like G,—
For thus inventing thing and title
Worship were that man's fit requital.
But if the common conscience must
Be ultimately judge, adjust

Its apt name to each quality
Already known,—I would decree
Worship for such mere demonstration
And simple work of nomenclature
Only the day I praised, not nature,
But Harvey, for the circulation.
I would praise such a Christ, with pride
And joy, that he, as none beside,
Had taught us how to keep the mind
God gave him, as God gave his kind,
Freer than they from fleshly taint :
I would call such a Christ our Saint,
As I declare our Poet, him
Whose insight makes all others dim :
A thousand poets pried at life,
And only one amid the strife
Rose to be Shakespeare : each shall take
His crown, I 'd say, for the world's sake—
Though some objected—" Had we seen
The heart and head of each, what screen
Was broken there to give them light,
While in ourselves it shuts the sight,
We should no more admire, perchance,
That these found truth out at a glance,
Than marvel how the bat discerns

Some pitch-dark cavern's fifty turns,
Led by a finer tact, a gift
He boasts, which other birds must shift
Without, and grope as best they can."
No, freely I would praise the man,—
Nor one whit more, if he contended
That gift of his from God descended.
Ah friend, what gift of man's does not?
No nearer something, by a jot,
Rise an infinity of nothings
Than one: take Euclid for your teacher:
Distinguish kinds: do crownings, clothings,
Make that creator which was creature?
Multiply gifts upon man's head,
And what, when all 's done, shall be said
But—the more gifted he, I ween!
That one 's made Christ, this other, Pilate,
And this might be all that has been,—
So what is there to frown or smile at?
What is left for us, save, in growth
Of soul, to rise up, far past both,
From the gift looking to the giver,
And from the cistern to the river,
And from the finite to infinity,
And from man's dust to God's divinity?

XVII

TAKE all in a word: the truth in
   God's breast
Lies trace for trace upon ours
   impressed:
Though he is so bright and we
   so dim,
We are made in his image to witness him:
And were no eye in us to tell,
Instructed by no inner sense,
The light of heaven from the dark of hell,
That light would want its evidence,—
Though justice, good and truth were still
Divine, if, by some demon's will,
Hatred and wrong had been proclaimed
Law through the worlds, and right misnamed.
No mere exposition of morality
Made or in part or in totality,
Should win you to give it worship, therefore:
And, if no better proof you will care for,
—Whom do you count the worst man upon
   earth?
Be sure, he knows, in his conscience, more
Of what right is, than arrives at birth
In the best man's acts that we bow before:

64

This last knows better—true, but my fact is,
'T is one thing to know, and another to practise.
And thence I conclude that the real God-
    function
Is to furnish a motive and injunction
For practising what we know already.
And such an injunction and such a motive
As the God in Christ, do you waive, and "heady,
High-minded," hang your tablet-votive .
Outside the fane on a finger-post?
Morality to the uttermost,
Supreme in Christ as we all confess,
Why need we prove would avail no jot
To make him God, if God he were not?
What is the point where himself lays stress?
Does the precept run " Believe in good,
In justice, truth, now understood
For the first time " ?—or, " Believe in me,
Who lived and died, yet essentially
Am Lord of Life " ? Whoever can take
The same to his heart and for mere love's sake
Conceive of the love,—that man obtains
A new truth ; no conviction gains
Of an old one only, made intense
By a fresh appeal to his faded sense.

XVIII

CAN it be that he stays inside?
Is the vesture left me to com-
    mune with?
Could my soul find aught to sing
    in tune with
Even at this lecture, if she tried?
Oh, let me at lowest sympathize
With the lurking drop of blood that lies
In the desiccated brain's white roots
Without throb for Christ's attributes,
As the lecturer makes his special boast!
If love 's dead there, it has left a ghost.
Admire we, how from heart to brain
(Though to say so strike the doctors dumb)
One instinct rises and falls again,
Restoring the equilibrium.
And how when the Critic had done his best,
And the pearl of price, at reason's test,
Lay dust and ashes levigable
On the Professor's lecture-table,—
When we looked for the inference and monition
That our faith, reduced to such condition,
Be swept forthwith to its natural dust-hole,—
He bids us, when we least expect it,

66

Take back our faith,—if it be not just whole,
Yet a pearl indeed, as his tests affect it,
Which fact pays damage done rewardingly,
So, prize we our dust and ashes accordingly!
" Go home and venerate the myth
I thus have experimented with—
This man, continue to adore him
Rather than all who went before him,
And all who ever followed after ! "—
Surely for this I may praise you, my brother !
Will you take the praise in tears or laughter ?
That 's one point gained : can I compass
     another ?
Unlearned love was safe from spurning—
Can 't we respect your loveless learning ?
Let us at least give learning honor !
What laurels had we showered upon her,
Girding her loins up to perturb
Our theory of the Middle Verb ;
Or Turk-like brandishing a scimitar
O'er anapæsts in comic-trimeter ;
Or curing the halt and maimed " Iketides,"
While we lounged on at our indebted ease :
Instead of which, a tricksy demon
Sets her at Titus or Philemon !

When ignorance wags his ears of leather
And hates God's word, 't is altogether;
Nor leaves he his congenial thistles
To go and browse on Paul's Epistles.
—And you, the audience, who might ravage
The world wide, enviably savage,
Nor heed the cry of the retriever,
More than Herr Heine (before his fever),—
I do not tell a lie so arrant
As say my passion's wings are furled up,
And, without plainest heavenly warrant,
I were ready and glad to give the world up—
But still, when you rub brow meticulous,
And ponder the profit of turning holy
If not for God's, for your own sake solely,
—God forbid I should find you ridiculous!
Deduce from this lecture all that eases you,
Nay, call yourselves, if the calling pleases you,
Christians,—abhor the deist's pravity,—
Go on, you shall no more move my gravity
Than, when I see boys ride a-cockhorse,
I find it in my heart to embarrass them
By hinting that their stick 's a mock horse,
And they really carry what they say carries
    them.
    68

XIX

O SAT I talking with my mind.
I did not long to leave the door
And find a new church, as before,
But rather was quiet and inclined
To prolong and enjoy the gentle
    resting
From further tracking and trying and testing.
" This tolerance is a genial mood ! "
(Said I, and a little pause ensued.)
"One trims the bark 'twixt shoal and shelf,
And sees, each side, the good effects of it,
A value for religion's self,
A carelessness about the sects of it.
Let me enjoy my own conviction,
Not watch my neighbor's faith with fretful-
    ness,
Still spying there some dereliction
Of truth, perversity, forgetfulness !
Better a mild indifferentism,
Teaching that both our faiths (though duller
His shine through a dull spirit's prism)
Originally had one color !
Better pursue a pilgrimage
Through ancient and through modern times

To many peoples, various climes,
Where I may see saint, savage, sage
Fuse their respective creeds in one
Before the general Father's throne!"

XX

'TWAS the horrible storm began
    afresh!
The black night caught me in
    his mesh,
Whirled me up, and flung me
    prone.
I was left on the college-step alone.
I looked, and far there, ever fleeting
Far, far away, the receding gesture,
And looming of the lessening vesture!—
Swept forward from my stupid hand,
While I watched my foolish heart expand
In the lazy glow of benevolence,
O'er the various modes of man's belief.
I sprang up with fear's vehemence.
Needs must there be one way, our chief
Best way of worship: let me strive
To find it, and when found, contrive
My fellows also take their share!
This constitutes my earthly care:
God's is above it and distinct.
For I, a man, with men am linked
And not a brute with brutes; no gain
That I experience, must remain

Unshared : but should my best endeavor
To share it, fail—subsisteth ever
God's care above, and I exult
That God, by God's own ways occult,
May—doth, I will believe—bring back
All wanderers to a single track.
Meantime, I can but testify
God's care for me—no more, can I—
It is but for myself I know;
The world rolls witnessing around me
Only to leave me as it found me;
Men cry there, but my ear is slow:
Their races flourish or decay
—What boots it, while yon lucid way
Loaded with stars divides the vault?
But soon my soul repairs its fault
When, sharpening sense's hebetude,
She turns on my own life! So viewed,
No mere mote's-breadth but teems immense
With witnessings of providence:
And woe to me if when I look
Upon that record, the sole book
Unsealed to me, I take no heed
Of any warning that I read !
Have I been sure, this Christmas Eve,

God's own hand did the rainbow weave,
Whereby the truth from heaven slid
Into my soul ?—I cannot bid
The world admit he stooped to heal
My soul, as if in a thunder-peal
Where one heard noise, and one saw
        flame,
I only knew he named my name :
But what is the world to me, for sorrow
Or joy in its censure, when to-morrow
It drops the remark, with just-turned head,
Then, on again, " That man is dead " ?
Yes, but for me—my name called,—drawn
As a conscript's lot from the lap's black
        yawn,
He has dipt into on a battle-dawn :
Bid out of life by a nod, a glance,—
Stumbling, mute-mazed, at nature's
        chance,—
With a rapid finger circled round,
Fixed to the first poor inch of ground
To fight from, where his foot was found ;
Whose ear but a minute since lay free
To the wide camp's buzz and gossipry—
Summoned, a solitary man,

To end his life where his life began,
From the safe glad rear, to the dreadful van!
Soul of mine, hadst thou caught and held
By the hem of the vesture !—

XXI

ND I caught
At the flying robe, and unrepelled
Was lapped again in its folds
    full-fraught
With warmth and wonder and
    delight,
God's mercy being infinite.
For scarce had the words escaped my tongue,
When, at a passionate bound, I sprung
Out of the wandering world of rain,
Into the little chapel again.

XXII

OW else was I found there, bolt
   upright
On my bench, as if I had never
   left it?
—Never flung out on the com-
   mon at night,
Nor met the storm and wedge-like cleft it,
Seen the raree-show of Peter's successor,
Or the laboratory of the Professor!
For the Vision, that was true, I wist,
True as that heaven and earth exist.
There sat my friend, the yellow and tall,
With his neck and its wen in the selfsame
      place;
Yet my nearest neighbor's cheek showed gall.
She had slid away a contemptuous space:
And the old fat woman, late so placable,
Eyed me with symptoms, hardly mistakable,
Of her milk of kindness turning rancid.
In short, a spectator might have fancied
That I had nodded, betrayed by slumber,
Yet kept my seat, a warning ghastly,
Through the heads of the sermon, nine in
      number,

And woke up now at the tenth and lastly.
But again, could such disgrace have happened?
Each friend at my elbow had surely nudged it;
And as for the sermon, where did my nap end?
Unless I heard it, could I have judged it?
Could I report as I do at the close,
First, the preacher speaks through his nose:
Second, his gesture is too emphatic:
Thirdly, to waive what 's pedagogic,
The subject-matter itself lacks logic:
Fourthly, the English is ungrammatic.
Great news! the preacher is found no Pascal,
Whom, if I pleased, I might to the task call
Of making square to a finite eye
The circle of infinity,
And find so all-but-just-succeeding!
Great news! the sermon proves no reading
Where bee-like in the flowers I bury me,
Like Taylor's, the immortal Jeremy!
And now that I know the very worst of him,
What was it I thought to obtain at first of him?
Ha! Is God mocked, as he asks?
Shall I take on me to change his tasks,
And dare, dispatched to a river-head
For a simple draught of the element,

Neglect the thing for which he sent,
And return with another thing instead ?—
Saying, " Because the water found
Welling up from underground,
Is mingled with the taints of earth,
While thou, I know, dost laugh at dearth,
And couldst, at wink or word, convulse
The world with the leap of a river-pulse,—
Therefore I turned from the oozings muddy,
And bring thee a chalice I found, instead :
See the brave veins in the breccia ruddy !
One would suppose that the marble bled.
What matters the water ? A hope I have
        nursed
The waterless cup will quench my thirst."
—Better have knelt at the poorest stream
That trickles in pain from the straitest rift !
For the less or the more is all God's gift,
Who blocks up or breaks wide the granite seam.
And here, is there water or not, to drink ?
I then, in ignorance and weakness,
Taking God's help, have attained to think
My heart does best to receive in meekness
That mode of worship, as most to his mind,
Where earthly aids being cast behind,

His All in All appears serene
With the thinnest human veil between,
Letting the mystic lamps, the seven,
The many motions of his spirit,
Pass, as they list, to earth from heaven.
For the preacher's merit or demerit,
It were to be wished the flaws were fewer
In the earthen vessel, holding treasure
Which lies as safe in a golden ewer;
But the main thing is, does it hold good
    measure?
Heaven soon sets right all other matters!—
Ask, else, these ruins of humanity,
This flesh worn out to rags and tatters,
This soul at struggle with insanity,
Who thence take comfort—can I doubt?—
Which an empire gained, were a loss without.
May it be mine! And let us hope
That no worse blessing befall the Pope,
Turn'd sick at last of to-day's buffoonery,
Of posturings and petticoatings,
Beside his Bourbon bully's gloatings
In the bloody orgies of drunk poltroonery!
Nor may the Professor forego its peace
At Gottingen presently, when, in the dusk

Of his life, if his cough, as I fear, should
    increase,
Prophesied of by that horrible husk—
When thicker and thicker the darkness fills
The world through his misty spectacles,
And he gropes for something more substantial
Than a fable, myth or personification,—
May Christ do for him what no mere man shall,
And stand confessed as the God of salvation!
Meantime, in the still recurring fear
Lest myself, at unawares, be found,
While attacking the choice of my neighbors
    round,
With none of my own made—I choose here!
The giving out of the hymn reclaims me ;
I have done : and if any blames me,
Thinking that merely to touch in brevity
The topics I dwell on, were unlawful,—
Or worse, that I trench, with undue levity,
On the bounds of the holy and the awful,—
I praise the heart, and pity the head of him,
And refer myself to Thee, instead of him,
Who head and heart alike discernest,
Looking below light speech we utter,
When frothy spume and frequent sputter
    80

Prove that the soul's depths boil in earnest!
May truth shine out, stand ever before us!
I put up pencil and join chorus
To Hepzibah Tune, without further apology,
The last five verses of the third section
Of the seventeenth hymn of Whitfield's Col-
    lection,
To conclude with the doxology.